DANGEROUS REGENCY ROMANCE

DANGEROUS REGENCY ROMANCE
By Cupideros

Cupideros Cupiderosbooks.com 2016

Copyright © 2016 by Cupideros

All rights reserved. This book or any portion thereof may not be reproduced or used in any manner whatsoever without the express written permission of the publisher except for the use of brief quotations in a book review or scholarly journal.

First Printing: January 4, 2017

ISBN: 978-1-365-65621-7

Cupiderosbooks.com
3524 Harvey Avenue, Apt. 207
Cincinnati, OH 45229

csfontaine927@hotmail.com   Ordering Information:

Special discounts are available on quantity purchases by corporations, associations, educators, and others. For details, contact the publisher at the above listed address.

U.S. trade bookstores and wholesalers: Please contact Cupideros Tel: (513) 680-9518 or email or csfontaine927@hotmail.com.

Dedication

To The Great God and The Great Goddess. May this work help born three-hole women and girls learn and think and grow in ways beneficial to the world.

Thank you. Without your support and patience, I would have never achieved my dream.

Contents

DANGEROUS REGENCY ROMANCE 1
   Copyright © 2016 by Cupideros 3
Dedication 4
Contents 5
Acknowledgements 6
Preface 1
Introduction 2
CHAPTER 1 3
CHAPTER 2 13
CHAPTER 3 22
CHAPTER 4 32
CHAPTER 5 36
CHAPTER 6 42

Acknowledgements

I thank all who purchase this novella and may it help inspire you to do great feminist works now and in the future.

Preface

Dangerous Regency Romance tackles critical thinking, love, and feminism in society through marriage relations. What will one do to maintain their marriage in a society that frowns upon it or does not even care about it. This book explores these topics.

Introduction

Regency Romance Novella
A Thriller Regency Romance
© Cupideros, October 4, 2016, 10:04 am EST
15,504 words

SHORT DESCRIPTION:
Two young dashing bachelor dukes make bet that would change their lives forever and the lives of their respective wives.

CHAPTER 1

ALBANY BACHELOR HOTEL
CARD GAMESTER ROOM
LONDON, ENGLAND
MONDAY, FEBRAUARY 21, 1814

There once were two dashing young dukes living in the Albany bachelor apartment for aristocrats, in London, England.

One, we shall call Duke Griffen Naismith; the other, we shall call Duke Rupert Steedmond. Names are unimportant in these types of stories. What is important is the import of the character's doings. For the two dukes met over a card game and came to a competitive conclusion, shocking to their bachelor male peers.

Duke Griffen Naismith said, "So you suppose yourself a better man, a better lover, and a better husband than I?"

"I do," said Duke Rupert Steedmond.

"That is saying a lot," murmured the small groups.

"I am," started Duke Rupert Steedmond," most excellent in all things dueling, picking racehorses at the Ascots, and even walking the high wire in the Circus Jim's."

"Walking the high wire, you say, Duke Rupert Steedmond? That's undignified sort of thing my good fellow, for a ton member. No. No, No. I propose--" Duke Griffen Naismith stopped for a second. "I propose we meet again, in private, and decide the terms of our competition."

Duke Rupert Steedmond turned to his other esteemed peers,

dukes, viscounts, marquees, and counts. "Not here? Not among our peers. Why who shall be the judge of our success?"

Smiling and smug, Duke Griffen Naismith replied. "Our peers and their peers."

Finally, Duke Rupert Steedmond understood and flashed a wry smile. "I do get your meaning," He chortled. "I do get your meaning." Duke Rupert Steedmond laughed.

Duke Griffen Naismith laughed.

All the other aristocrats in the ton bachelor Albany apartments started laughing. But they had no real factual clue what Duke Griffen Naismith meant. They only liked the idea; somehow, they'd get to decide the winner.

Later on, Duke Griffen Naismith and Duke Rupert Steedmond met in private, in the shire of Devon, foreign to the both of them. They were not well-known and went unnoticed.

The Two Dukes decided these terms: Duke Griffen Naismith chooses the marriage partner for Duke Rupert Steedmond. Duke Rupert Steedmond would return the favor to Duke Griffen Naismith.

Smiling and smug, Duke Griffen Naismith said, "She is beautiful and probably virginal, too. Her composure is ton like. Her looks can launch a regional skirmish, perhaps. something between two minor powers of state. She loves to wear the color of peach and looks fine it, I must say. But," Duke Griffen Naismith paused and rubbed his bare chin.

Duke Rupert Steedmond impatient to know his future wife, said, "Get on with it man."

"Do not fret, my good fellow, at the competition none stands in your way. She is nonton." Duke Griffen Naismith paused again, adding finally, "She is a mulatto."

Duke Rupert Steedmond gasped in horror.

"Before you object and give me the victory outright, Duke Rupert Steedmond, given all that it is about this particular mulatto woman, I want to add, if she were not so slightly mixed, I'd marry her myself. And only in the sunlight would anyone notice Constantia's difference of race, Duke Rupert Steedmond. I think you have the far easier choice in a wife than I."

Duke Rupert Steedmond wanted to hand over the large sum of money. Someone thousand pounds right then and there, but as their meeting was private, he figured who would know? "I have to marry her and stay married?"

Duke Griffen Naismith in a stoic voice replied, "What good is a wager broken?"

"That given as it is," Duke Rupert Steedmond started slowly, thinking, pondering the future wife for his peer. "That given as it is, I've got a most excellent choose for you, Duke Griffen Naismith, a ton, woman, not too ugly and not too pretty either, who turned into a spinster some three years prior. Spinster Lady Elinor Watson is well off financially; her dowry could launch a war." Duke Rupert Steedmond chuckled.

"Spinster! You've chosen for me to marry a spinster! This spinster Lady Elinor Watson of Hampshire. Crikey!" retorted Duke Griffen Naismith. "You are a sly, mean sort of fellow. For, I have to live with this woman the rest of my life."

"We," Duke Rupert gestured his forefinger to himself and then Duke Griffen, have to stay married," Duke Rupert Steedmond corrected.

"It is fair." Smiling and smug, Duke Griffen Naismith simply shrugged his shoulders.

Duke Rupert Steedmond asked, "But when shall we declare the winner?"

Confident Duke Griffen Naismith gave his reply. "Six years hence from today's date, February 21, 1820." Duke Griffen Naismith hurriedly added, "You are free to end the bet right now, Duke Rupert."

Duke Rupert Steedmond said, "That's a long, long time. Napoleon will surely be defeated by then."

Duke Griffen Naismith replied, "We hope, Duke Rupert Steedmond. We hope. And sadly, King George III will have passed away by that time, too."

The two dukes shook hands on the mattered and both pulled out Cuban cigars and drank a toast. "To Marriage, Adventure, and Mystery."

Duke Rupert Steedmond wickedly replied, "Most assuredly, the spinster's mystery."

Duke Griffen Naismith cautiously replied, "The brazen mulatto mystery."

Both Dukes concluded their bet after vowing not a word to a soul, other than God and not in a confessional sense. No one must know of our reason for marrying the woman of our choice. He who tells forfeits the bet.

And so, it was the two Dukes wooed and won their respective women and married them in two separate ceremonies. Duke Griffen Naismith married Lady Elinor Watson of Hampshire.

Duke Rupert Steedmond married the mulatto woman, Constantia, who served as a servant woman for Countess Heathcote in London.

Both feigned surprise at the marriage choice of the other. They moved out of the Albany apartments, for staying there merely increased the chances of revealing the "why" of their bet choices. Each settled down to a life of marriage, talking strolls in Hyde Park, visiting the Covent Theater with their wives, attending museums and country dance balls.

***

YEAR TWO: MAY 14, 1814:
ASSEMBLY ROOMS ALMACKS
KING STREET
LONDON, ENGLAND
EVENING, SATURDAY, MAY 15, 1814

"I don't see why I can't attend the Assembly's of Almack, Countess Dorothea Benckendorff. Why you yourself are a foreigner, a Russian and look how quickly you have risen in ton society!" Duke Rupert Steedmond said to the attractive, dark curly locks Society Patroness of Almacks. Her oval face and long nose, that mark of Russian beauty, and her big black eyes invited one to fall inside of them, reveal all your secrets.

"Dear Duke Rupert Steedmond. I understand your disappointment. Russia has had disappointments. But these are things to get over and get on with life. I am sure many balls and dances will accept Duchess Constantia. Oh, Dear, there is Duke Seabrook. He must have something important to say to me."

Duke Rupert Steedmond smoldered as he and Duchess Constantia retreated from the Almack's on King Street.

"Don't worry, Duke Rupert. One day we shall be full members of ton society, but right now all I want is to be married to you." She kissed him. Small random gasps escaped the crowd but by this time, Duke Rupert Steedmond's marriage to the mulatto was no longer the gossip scandal it had been in the beginning. Because Duchess Constantia conducted herself with the higher class and her intellect seemed no different than the other ton women. Duchess Constantia had been a servant woman in the household of Countess Heathcote from London. Duchess Constantia found all things ton worthy of acquiring. Her beauty, her light-light skinned beauty reminded one of an Italian princess in fact.

Outside Duke Rupert saw Duke Griffen Naismith and his duchess exiting their brougham carriage. Everyone clapped and spoke.'

"Why there is Duke Griffen Naismith. That most honorable ton man."

"A true spirit of compassion and class. Elinor Watson seemed doom to a life of loneliness."

"This is proof," said another Marquess, "That God exists and protects those who are kind at heart."

Duke Griffen Naismith and Duchess Elinor Watson walked pass Duke Rupert Steedmond and Duchess Constantia, and Duke Rupert Steedmond, in his righteous angry mood, almost didn't speak."

"Why if it isn't Duke Griffen Naismith old friend. Have I

offended you?"

"No. Not you. No, not at all my good fellow." Duke Rupert Steedmond looked backward slightly at Countess Benckendorff talking to Duke Seabrook and her husband, Count Lieven, the Russian ambassador. "Just a small matter, actually. I won't fret over it."

"Where is that smiling, smug Duke of long ago?" dug Duke Griffen Naismith into Duke Rupert Steedmond's feelings and intellect.

Flashing a bright smile that brought his Duchess Constantia to a happier countenance, Duke Rupert Steedmond said, "I was think about you the other day, and here we met at the Almack's."

"Aren't you going in?" Duke Griffen said, smiling and smug. I and Duchess Elinor plan on having a good time. He showed Duke Rupert his voucher.

Duchess Constantia gasped for Duke Rupert never got a voucher or rather could not obtain one in the proper place. Thinking this a mistake he decided to show up in person. Perhaps Countess Benckendorff's instructions were a mistake. Duke Rupert was certainly ton. Duke Rupert chortled and laughed. He shook his head. "No actually we have to attend another ball. Someone new came into town the hostess wants me to meet."

Duke Griffen Naismith said after receiving a telling glance from his once spinster wife, Duchess Elinor. "Do not fret, my good fellow." Duke Griffen slapped Duke Rupert on the upper arm. "Cheer up. Rumor has it Napoleon is about to be defeated at Waterloo."

"You do say. I've heard similar rumors. What a pleasant surprise," Duke Rupert commented, feeling better at having met his old friend. It appeared to Duke Rupert that Duke Griffen got the better end of their bet. Duke Griffen Naismith in good standing in the ton went up. Duke Rupert's own reputation went down. Duke Rupert found this not a sufficient reason for calling off the secret bet, however. He rather loved his mulatto wife, Constania, and her talents in bed wiped out the memories of his earlier unmarried dalliances. Yes, he was happy, in a sort of satisfied, mysterious way. "To marriage, adventure, and mystery!" Duke Rupert Steedmond replied,ending the conversation. He chortled for good measure.

Smiling and smug Duke Griffen replied, "Yes, to marriage adventure and mystery."

The two Dukes departed and went on with their lives. Later they celebrated the war's end at a big party, not the Almacks, but another important ton hostess, Duke Rupert and his mulatto duchess were invited. At this country dance ball, Duke Rupert Steedmond found himself a rather curious oddity, or shall we say his mulatto wife was the curious oddity. Everyone well expected her to trip up here or there on some fact of British history or pronouncing a word or even a faux pas at dancing. None of these things happened and the mystery of when Duchess Constantia's would faux pas remained a hidden novelty of ton society.

Whereas with Duke Griffen Naismith the mysterious novelty remained when would he tire of his spinster? For many assumed, she lacked qualities of love and lust. However, Duchess Elinor was a normal woman who happened not to be married at a young age. Her war chest bought improvement to Duke Griffen's Manor House. Expansions followed in land purchases and of course, that meant higher more servants to work the land. Duke Griffen grew trees and fruits in Kentshire. His well-off investment, funded by Duchess Elinor's war chest dowry which increase double fold by the end of the year one alone. Duke Griffen Naismith was happier ton man by far. "I love you, Duchess Constantia. You're proof spinsters are a myth anda slur."

Duchess Elinor had tears in her small blue eyes, eyes that should have been larger given her triangular shaped face. Her nose was a little, too, long, but if you took in the bigger picture of her long brunette hair, thick and shiny, she had a special charming beauty after all.
Nevertheless, things in both camps, hidden of course, bothered both Duke Griffen Naismith and Duke Rupert Steedmond. We shall discuss Duke Griffen Naismith's annoyances first, because most readers will assume Duke Rupert Steedmond had the more difficult

time of this bet. In fact, Duke Griffen Naismith fought off urges to quit his marriage six months into the secret agreement. See, Duke Griffen Naismith rather always fancied the pretty ladies and as Duchess Elinor was on the rather modest side of the beauty fence; he wanted to taste other beauties on the side. He fought off these moments, night, and day, especially at the balls. Those precious few moments when Duchess Elinor disappeared to do ton women's stuff helping out the country dance ball hostess brought him the most pain. One is rather content in one's private quarters, but imagine being thrown into an environment with the most stunning women of the age. Women young vibrant. Women whose blooms have not fell off their face. Take for example Lady Ava St. George, her effervescent personality drew most men like honey on bread, for even a hater of bread. Her bubbly voice and excellent dancing, draws one's mind wonders how things in bed would be with Ava. Duke Griffen Naismith never doubted, once spinster Duchess Elinor, showed him higher sights. But, and but was the question, Duke Griffen Naismith always wondered about the younger ton women. Women so young they did not need perfume. Debuting women, naturally young, exuded an aroma of lust and desire. Duke Griffen even wondered about Duke Rupert Steedmond's mulatto wife. Duke Griffen Naismith knew it was wrong, but he wondered how to stay married to Duchess Elinor until 1820. Who knows what will happen in such a long time? Duke Griffen Naismith had offers. Duke Griffen had lots of offers. Offers he never had in his bachelor days at the Albany Apartments for rogue, adventuresome ton male aristocrats like himself. These ton bachelors sympathized with his plight. Marrying a spinster was charity they said. They constantly badgered Duke Griffen, why he did it? They remembered the bet from one year ago and inquired: Is this the bet between you and Duke Rupert Steedmond?"

Smiling and smug, Duke Griffen Naismith replied. "On your life, do you think I'd marry a spinster to win money, to boost my pride?" I am a ton. I do things out of a noble sense of honor. No woman of good character, wealth, standing in our ton community should be sequestered because of her age. Each of us will age one day. Our wives, my good fellows, will age. Our children will age. Ton society will age as a new crop of younger ton push us to the sidelines and chairs in the country dance balls throughout England," Duke Griffen Naismith lied. Well, half lied. A well put half-lie. Duke Griffen married Duchess Elinor for her internal qualities and her wealth. Now, if only her external beauty stopped nagging him.

This nagging, to be honest, was Duke Griffen's own making. Many a man divorced and married again to a woman of the exact same age as Duchess Elinor. So why the gossip of spinsters still attached to her name? What did Duchess Elinor do wrong in her prior life to make her become a spinster? Many disturbing questions arose in Duke Griffen as he searched for an excuse to do what his wicked heart and loins wanted to do all along—marry a young and vibrant, rich, respected, intelligent ton wife. At this point, his first choice of marriage dried away, long gone from him.

Better to enjoy the fruits growing on your side of the fence than to fancy fruits on the other side. They will not taste any sweeter for having hopped the fence, trespassed on another's land, and then bitof the forbidden fruits.

In Duke Rupert Steedmond's camp, his problems were obvious. Most accepted grudgingly, with reservations, after looking aslant, and questioned indirectly, in small questions, behind his back, if Duchess Constantia was ton worthy. When they were alone in their big Manor House on the north side of London, Duke Rupert Steedmond was happy as a little boy with a room full of toys.

Duchess Constantia marveled at how happy Duke Rupert Steedmond was alone in her presence. They played and frolicked more like to neighborhood children, boy and girl, left alone to their devices and plans. They did all kinds of things nonton. That sat on the floor in Duke Rupert Steedmond's large bedroom and ate crackers and jam. They read books to each other late into the night, and not the classics or high literature mind you. They took baths together. He would finger comb her long black hair, brushing it with his fingers down the lightly tanned skin of her back. Together, they climbed trees at night out in the formal garden. She told him tales, grandmom tales about the West Indies and Caribbean's slaves and pirates and stolen loot. Things she never saw in her life, but persisted in her background from ancient relatives long, gone, and dead. Duchess Constantia was a mysterious woman and entirely entertaining. She brought entertainment as her wealth, not poundsand coins.

This would be enough for Duke Rupert Steedmond. Except for the persistent fact, he had guests drop over. Their parlor doorman announced this ambassador, or this Member of Parliament or merchant or land seller, speaking of big tracts of land available in Louisiana territory forfeited by Emperor Napoleon some years back. People, who upon seeing his Duchess, halted, gasped, found their thoughts frozen, if they'd met her by the door, in the light. And Duke Rupert Steedmond lived in constantly annoyance of these important people withdrawing their support if his Duchess Constantia accompanied them to the door.

Thank God for doormen, main servants of the household doing these duties. Nevertheless, Duke Rupert Steedmond wanted to merge the two worlds together. How? How? How? Might I do such a thing? See, dear reader, Duke Rupert Steedmond never thought about Duke Griffen Naismith's wife, so Duke Rupert had the advantage.

Only if, Duke Rupert Steedmond could stop thinking about ton society, he'd be happy. Then he would be truly happy. Thoughts crossed Duke Rupert Steedmond's mind of sailing abroad, away from England. He wondered if that was in their secret bet—fair and legal to sail away. He trained as the barrister, and as a lawyer, he sought ways to wiggle out of his bet without being declared the loser. He laughed, too, hard and chortled, too, confidently to let Duke Griffen Naismith win this secret bet.

Neither man knew the other wanted to break the bet, however.

Both men held a one-hundred percent belief, given their flawed marriage mates, sooner or later the other ton male, in the bet, wanted to bolt to freedom. Perhaps, Duke Rupert Steedmond, thought, I can encourage Duke Griffen Naismith to concede defeat first.

On the southern side of London, Duke Griffen Naismith thought the same thing. What events to manipulate in Duke Rupert Steedmond's life to make him give up the secret bet.

CHAPTER 2

YEAR THREE CIRCUS JIM'S
LONDON, ENGLAND
WEDNESDAY, MAY 15, 1816

Shouting over the loud crowd, Rupert Steedmond asked, "How do you like the circus, Duchess Constantia?"

People walked about. Performers not performing smiled. Refreshments servants came around to see if anyone wanted food. A man walked by on tall six-foot stilts, his eyes looking over the seated crowd's wide-spread eyes.

"You're not really going to go on the high wire. Please don't Rupert. What will I do if you hurt yourself or die?"

"You've met my lawyer. You would be well-taken care of. My will includes you, first. You have an annuity. I've even entitled the land so it goes to you as well. That, my dear cannot be broken, by anyone in my family."

"Crikey!" Duchess Constantia said having now adopted the term for herself. She had been a member of the ton for three years. Even though she wasn't fully accepted, she felt comfortable receiving the salutations from ton and nonton. Things were not so bad. Some nonton from India arrived as well. "Come and sit down. Take off those ridiculous high wire walking clothes. They're, too, tight dear. Be conservative for Heaven's sake. And no more about your Banbury Tales of my receiving an inheritance and wills. Emma Hamiliton, Lord Nelson's wife died penniless in France. Did he not ask the British government to see after his wife? Didn't he will her funds and house to live like a noble?"

Rupert Steedmond had not sat. He put one foot on the bleachers a foot away from his wife. He leaned on one knee. His leg and arm and chest muscles flexed in the skintight calisthenics suit. "You worry, too, much, my dear, Duchess Constantia. You are getting like Duke Griffen Naismith," Rupert Steedmond chortled. He tossed back his head and laughed. "Amy Lyons, a Blacksmith's daughter, started out as a prostitute." Rupert Steedmond rolled his right hand out as if making a business proposition. "I suppose, she'd been a blacksmith, if she bore the strength of her dad. But that as it is, born female, she became a prostitute and after passing from several men found herself employed by Lord Nelson."

Duchess Constantia tightened her Pomona green bonnet around her head. "Crikey! Rupert. None of this changes the situation."

"Honestly, love, I do get your meaning," Rupert chortled. "But listen. Lord Nelson left his wife like a sunken ship for Emma. Amy changed her name to Emma." Rupert Steedmond stroked his mulatto wife's dark long hair. "You, however, are neither a former prostitute, nor a wife hopper." He hugged her to him, as if the noisy circus crowd cheered and elephants now blew their horns. While an undistracted a circus performer, in tights much like Rupert Steedmond's, only with sparkles on it, did flips on the moving elephants back circling the rings under the big top.

Duchess Constantia's face went through several quick emotions. She said nothing.

"You never liked me conservative, Duchess Constantia." happy Duke Rupert chortled and laughed. He chortled and laughed. "This is a time for adventure, we are young healthy—"

"And pregnant!"

Duke Rupert Steedmond stopped moving around, doing calisthenics, warming up. "You're pregnant!"

Duke Rupert slowly sat down beside his wife.

"Four months, but my family never loses a child." Duchess Constantia warned and waited anxiously.

"Crikey! This is something to worry about." Duke Rupert Steedmond paused. He'd have to think of something sooner than expected to make Duke Griffen Naismith quit the bet, given this change. "This is wonderful. A little Duke Rupert Steedmond or Duchess Constantia."

Duchess Constantia giggled. She rotated her shoulders from

side to side. "If I know heredity correctly, the child will be a mixture of both of us." Her brown eyes widen when she answered.

"Yes, yes, of course, my dear. You, hmmm. That given as it is, I guess, I should forego the high-wire act, my love." He sat down on the first-row bleachers with his mulatto wife, Duchess Constantia. "Wouldn't be a nasty jar for our little son to lose his dad before laying eyes on him?" Duke Rupert grabbed Duchess Constantia and hugged her shoulders. "Is a kiss now, too, conservative?"

"I don't think anyone cares."

Duke Rupert Steedmond kisses Duchess Constantia in a brief passionate embrace. "You make me so happy, My Love. We are so happy here. No one even notices you. Everyone accepts you, even the ringmaster Jim."

"That's because this is a society of misfits and oddities. I admit I am an oddity."

Duchess Constantia turned away and noticed a woman struggling with a man wearing a coat and tails, and top hat. "Dear that woman," she pointed her fan toward the opening going into the back circus tents, areas for performers only, "she seems to be a cat in hell without claws." The young performer looked no more than eighteen. She carried a big hoop, but suddenly let it fall the dirt, as the gentleman grabbed her. He pulled her close.

Duke Rupert Steedmond watched for a second. He smiled. Then he stopped smiling as he and his mulatto wife watched the man pulling the unwilling woman toward him for a kiss.

"Duke Rupert. Do something," Duchess Constantia pleaded.

Duke Rupert watched what the man's waters, his actions. Duke Rupert Steedmond's face turned to disgust as the situation continued. He turned a darker shade of red, and hopped up, from his sitting position looking over his wife's shoulders at the woman in hot water or as a cat in hell without claws, he said, "I'll be back in a second."

Strutting, and determined to change the young female performer's fate, Duke Rupert Steedmond soon confronted the man. "I don't think the young woman likes your company, Sir."

"How dare you even speak to me? I am a viscount! You are a nobody performer. Ton can do what they want here."

"I don't think so," Duke Rupert replied, balling up his fist. The viscount let the woman's shoulders go.

She rubbed her shoulders. She was petite and had blonde hair and a shapely figure.

The viscount added, "This circus is a covey, a collection of whores."

Duke Rupert Steedmond surprised the man by replying, "Do you want to settle this in the Norman tradition?"

Shocked, but still angered the viscount halted his speech. "You are ton?"

"The very best of ton, Duke Rupert Steedmond."

"Thank you, Sir," gushed the young woman. Who then scurried away to the back dressing rooms.

"You haven't heard the last of me. I know Jim--"

"I know Jim, too!" Duke Rupert said cutting off the rude viscount.

The viscount trampled off and took a side exit from the circus tent.

Circus Jim came up wearing his sparkly top hat. "Duke Rupert Steedmond." Circus Jim's face showed annoyance.

"That gentleman put one your performer into hot water. She was young, a cat in hell without claws."

"Some girls do what they want to do, Duke Rupert Steedmond."

Confused, Duke Rupert asked, "What do you mean?"

"Girls here come from the streets. From bad places, I give them a chance for a different life. But sometimes, their life finds them."

Duke Rupert Steedmond chortled. "Well, I just put her past behind her."

"Do not do that again, Duke Rupert."

"What!" Aghast, Duke Rupert responded, "Jim. We're friends." Duke Rupert turned to the entrance behind the circus tent. He pointed to her hoop's mark in the dirt. "She needed help."

Circus Jim tipped his sparkly top hat back and showed his sweaty dark straight hair sticking to his scalp. "This circus survives on support like that viscount's." Circus Jim said in a solemn, serious manner.

Duke Rupert waved his hands. "My wife saw that rude viscount--all ton are not like him, Circus Jim. You've got to know that," Duke Rupert said with a big smile. "My wife saw him and--. I'll pay you whatever that viscount's support was. I'll write you a check."

Jim shook his head, no. "And what about the next, count, marquess or duke who comes seeking out these doxies. You willing to pay for all those other ton's lost support? I need ton support to keep this circus going."

"You're doing great, Circus Jim." Duke Rupert Steedmond pointed to the crowded wooden stands full of people, more numerous than minutes before. "It's more crowded than when I and Duchess Constantia first came in Jim."

"Many though they are, their funds are limited. With a few ton's support, I can keep the circus going for a year, two years."

"You're telling me--telling me, I did something wrong."

"I'm not trying to tell you anything, you are ton, Duke Rupert Steedmond. I know my place in society."

"I'm not threating you, Circus Jim." Duke Rupert reached out and touched Circus Jim's shoulders. "I can here to show my wife the high-wire act."

Circus Jim simply shook his head no.

Duke Rupert in his enthusiasm to tell Circus Jim about his wife's pregnancy missed the quiet gesture. "I was all prepared to walk the high-wire, when I found out she's pregnant."

His normally jovial voice came out flat. "That's great, Duke Rupert."

"So--I--can't--walk the high-wire--after all." Duke Rupert Steedmond, finally, understood the deep consternation in his old friend's big oval face. His heavy big bulbous nose and yellow teeth, and small brown eyes spoke volumes. Rethinking his actions, Duke Rupert Steedmond didn't like the interpretation, Circus Jim placed on those actions. He'd done the right thing in interfering. Duchess Constantia noticed the young woman in trouble. As an outsider, he agreed to his outsider mulatto's wife sensitivity. Something was wrong and he did something about it! Now Circus Jim acted like this!

"I've never been one to go along with crowds. I never figured you, Jim, to be one of those crowd fellows."

"All my people have to eat and perform. Without food, our performances would be lousy. No one would come."

The nasty jar, Circus Jim placed Duke Rupert Steedmond in all came down to one thing, his wife's high values. And there was no way of getting rid of her high values. She'd never forget how some has mistreated her as a mulatto. The Almack's cut direct. The cut indirect of some ton members who disapproved of his wife. Cut indirect, turning away, and acting like they somehow missed him and his mulatto wife was one thing, but now Circus Jim was cutting him indirect. "I won't come here anymore, Jim, if that satisfies you."

Circus Jim nodded in sadness.

"But I will continue to speak highly of you."

"As I will of you, Duke Rupert Steedmond."

Duke Rupert Steedmond walked back slow, and almost befogged. "Uh." Duke Rupert paused.

His wife brown eyes searched for the meaning of his lamentable face. "What is it, dear? What did your friend Circus Jim say?" She reached out and grabbed Duke Rupert's hand, pulling him down beside her.

"He said--" Duke Rupert shook his head. "He said in so many words, I wasn't his friend anymore. Mention some balmy on the crumpet idea, I should not have interfered with the viscount and that young woman."

"Crazy idea, you--you shouldn't have--but he was hurting her, threatening her?"

Duke Rupert Steedmond grabbed his bag holding his dress clothes. "She was a doxie. Most of the girl here are doxies, Circus Jim said. That viscount had some unfinished business with her."

"You mean she had to service--be with the viscount."

"I don't think that, Duchess Constantia." Duke Rupert Steedmond tied up his clothing bag. "No ton should treat a woman that way. We're better than that. Circus Jim seemed very worried of the viscount's support, the ton's support to run the circus." Duke

Rupert Steedmond motion waved to all the people in the crowd. "Apparently all of these people, commoners, are not enough to support him. Uhhhh, forget it, Duchess Constantia. I'm soon to be a dad. I don't need to be walking a high wire. We'll go to the Covent Garden Theater." Duke Rupert chortled loudly. "I want you to see England's most famous and favorite clown, Joseph Grimaldi, playingin *Harlequin and Mother Goose*. I'll change in the men's room."

"But your clothes will be all wrinkled. I wanted to see the circus, Duke Rupert Steedmond. Not you walking that dreadful high wire."

"Yes, but who will see in our private booth, and at a clown show, who will care." Duke Rupert Steedmond chortled again. "Forget the circus. We don't need the circus. It's not a respectable ton thing to do anyway." He pulled her up from the wooden benches, as the circus began. "Did I tell you I love you in Pomona green?"

"It's the fashion color of the year. Mrs. Maud Bellingham, the clothier said."

"Grab your parasol and we'll get some tea in Soho-"

Duchess Constantia flashed Duke Rupert a horror look.

"Crikey! You will get us some tea in Soho while I wait in the brougham carriage."

Duchess Constantia relaxed her face as they began walking down aisle leading out the circus.

"Remember, Duchess Constantia, my love, don't pother. You have more serious things to think about now." Duke Rupert gently placed his hand on his mulatto's wife's belly as they entered the sunlight.

Duke Rupert Steedmond's frustration escaped with a big sigh as he watched his lovely mulatto wife go for tea at the small shop. It wasn't her fault. She assessed the situation correctly. Circus Jim, his old friend, over identified with ton. Everyone wants money, easy money, money in large amounts. And one day, Duke Rupert Steedmond, hoped Jim got that money, that collection of monkeys to make the difference between surviving day after day, to being able to rest assured night after night. Ton didn't have to work. They did have other problems, pride, competition amongst themselves for starters.

Duke Rupert Steedmond thought back to three years ago. When he and Duke Griffen Naismith made the bet how pride got to him. Lead him down this road of dwindling friends and associates, who supported him in private. However, in public, they eschewed him. He determined to win this bet, now, not only for his own sake, but for his wife's pride. She kept it a closely guarded secret, but Duchess Constantia had pride. Duke Rupert Steedmond laughed to himself. She was not missish at all. She looked at life like he did, the big picture, not the short temporary one. Truth and justice mattered to her. Excellent qualities for rearing his children. Her confidence in protecting another woman, how did he put a pound sign on that awareness? Maybe she came to him on a bet driven by the pride of two arrogant ton men, on the surface, but certainly providence provided him the loving help meet and wife best suited for his untraditional innerself.

All the ton had pride, arrogance, too, and sometimes they let these qualities prove to the common folk on thing: ton and common folk came from the same stock, Adam and Eve, the parents of the fall. Duchess Constantia fit like a glove the purpose the Creator had in store for him. To teach him to treat everyone as an equal.

In the Covent Garden Theater, Duke Rupert Steedmond and Duchess Constantia talked quietly. Sometimes they giggled at the funny scenes, but mostly they held hands. Joy, privacy, the distance from the crowd, adjusted the ton's view of Duchess Constantia. From their theater booth, she looked perfectly wife. Even from the distance below, people could imagine her eyes to be blue.

More than a few waved to her, even after looking up at them through spyglasses. Her Pomona green empire dress went over very well. And Duchess Constantia waved her conservative fan back to them.

Duchess Constantia leaned a tiny bit, the heart-engraved busk in the front of her corset, making it nearly impossible to bend, further and she whispered into Duke Rupert's ear. "I understand you stayed at the Albany Bachelor apartments, before our marriage."

Duke Rupert Steedmond leaned back away from her in mock surprise. "I was a bachelor, not a rake. And I'll tell you my love that bachelor life has no happiness compared to being married."

Duke Rupert Steedmond kissed his wife and wondered now. Had someone mentioned about the bet? What if they had? Surely only the men knew and they kept a tight lid on such manly matters.

"I admit to being a little curious as to how you choose me," Duchess Constantia urged in a coy fashion.

"God brought you to my attention; no matter what we think God brings things into and out of our lives."

Duchess Constantia giggled and replied, "But there is the devil, too."

"That given as it is, let him try to break us up. I'll go to loggerheads against anyone trying separate our hearts and affections."

And for Duke Rupert Steedmond that meant one particular thing, to put into motion his plans to make Duke Griffen Naismith lose the wager as soon as possible. Then his love for Duchess Constantia retained no cloud of confusion or hint of disregard for her as a plaything. All would know when he stays married, he meant to love his wife, purely because he loved her and nothing else.

CHAPTER 3

YEAR THREE
DUKE GRIFFEN NAISMITH'S MANOR HOUSE
FORMAL GARDEN
SOUTHERN, LONDON, ENGLAND
SATURDAY, MAY 30, 1816

Duke Griffen Naismith rolled a fat juicy apple in his palm as he talked, "So have you heard the latest, my friend, Sebastian?" Two birds with brown and black coloring flitted by and landed in the trees some ten feet distance from the white garden table and three chairs around it. Small chatter drifted over the Hah-Hah wall across the long, spacious wide green lawn before them.

Sometimes Duke Griffen Naismith called Sebastian, his friend, Seb. Sebastian Howe was a conservative fellow who advised Duke Griffen Naismith on matters of stocks, industry, and business. He quietly disapproved of the spinster marriage, but kept his tongue guild into golden silence. He held and looked strangely before putting a banana back into the large silver fruit bowl on the white garden table. He smiled and grabbed a grapefruit. Quickly, though, he realized one hand insufficient for handling the yellow fruit. "Two hands I suppose."
"Two hands," said Duchess Elinor before she put another dark-purple grape into her small mouth.
Duke Griffen picked up a small fruit knife. Slicing the apple in half, he put the larger half down on the white plate with birch leaves of Saxon blue and Devonshire brown, named after notorious Georgiana Cavendish, Duchess of Devonshire who passed ten years prior. "In the spirit of Georgiana Cavendish, and our scandalous peers and their peers, Beau Brummell has fled England for France."
"You don't say," Sebastian responded, as he sliced a neat triangle of grapefruit and popped it into his mouth. He chewed. "I guess money talks or the lack of monkeys talk."

"That Bow Street window fellow with the famous wit and penchant for rudeness." Elinor gave a wry smile. "God does exists! He was always a thorn in my side. He cut direct me as if I were a half-world soon as I became a spinster."

"That would be Beau. Friend of Prince Regent and in debts to friends and his admirers alike." Sebastian let a quiet laugh escape from his lips. "But Duchess Elinor, we have no proof God caused Beau's downfall. More likely his own arrogance and poor card playing skills."

Duke Griffen Naismith had several cubes of apple on his plate, but he kept cutting from his apple half.

Duchess Elinor took the jab politely. She waved a dismissive hand. The two never agreed, she and Sebastian. "I care not what force brought Dandyism to ruin, God or Devil."

They all chortled in a rare moment of relaxing their demeanors.

"With a tolerable economy, I think a single man can dress as I do for L800," Duke Griffen remarked, sending another round of laughter escaping from their lips.

"I know a craftsman who makes L52 in one year." Duchess Elinor shook her head. It was obvious more things exist that entertained the world than her odd successful marriage with Duke Griffen Naismith.

In his understated tone of voice, Sebastian added, "How did such a man get in charge of ton society? To actually be influencing how we dressed, what we ate and thought?"

"I don't know. I don't know," Duchess Elinor said with tears of joy almost coming out of her eyes.

"This is, too, funny. France. Why didn't we just send Buck Brummell over to France in 1807. We'd save a lot of lives as Buck Brummell got the French army dressing up so much and so factiously, they'd never win one battle." Duke Griffen laughed. "I shouldn't be laughing so much. It's not my style. Ahem."

Sebastian stopped laughing, too. "We are ton. Someone has to keep us following God and laying down the conservative path in things."

"Right." Duke Griffen gave a smug smile. "I will never forgive him for cut directing you, Duchess Elinor. I didn't have anything to do with his downfall. But I am pleased nonetheless."

"So must be the Regent Prince," commented Sebastian and chuckled twice, suppressing laughter.

"'Alvanley, who is your fat friend?' he asked, referring to the Prince." Duke Griffen finally popped the square piece of apple into his mouth and grinned.

Lady Duchess Elinor and Sebastian could not contain their laughter again. They burst out laughing.

His mouth full of juicy apple, Duke Griffen nodded his mirthful approval.

"At least he kept his pants tightly girdled," Duchess Elinor suggested. "Georgiana Cavendish certainly had trouble there."

Their lighthearted, starry-eye laughter began again.

Duke Griffen Naismith hastened to pop two and one more square of apple bits to halt his laughter. But the smile lines around his eyes showed the depth of good times the three were having.

They sat quietly. Recovering.

"When you're ready," Duke Griffen suggested, "I have another funny bit of news. This closer to home."

"Than Beau!" Sebastian asked?

They all began laughing, again.

"Remember, Duchess Elinor, that fellow I said 'Do not fret to when he got cut direct by Assembly's of Almack, Countess Dorothea Benckendorff?"

"I remember him."

Sebastian remained quiet.

"All right fellow. I used to play cards with him. But having giving up the card trade, after becoming more aware of its destructive influence on men," Duke Griffen halted a chuckled, "I heard. He's lost another of his associates. Circus Jim."

"Circus Jim?" Sebastian asked.

"Circus Jim runs the circus here," Duke Griffen added clarification. "And seems one of their doxies had unfinished business with a viscount."

"Do we know his name?" Duchess Elinor inquired.

"Ahem. No, I do not. But the fellow I befriended at Assembly of Almacks, outside anyway, he used to walk the high wire."

Sebastian quietly threw back his head. But said nothing.

Smiling smug, Duke Griffen Naismith pointed to Sebastian. "Seb, you know who I'm talking about."

Duchess Elinor smiled a half wry, smile. Then suddenly she said, "The fellow with the mulatto wife!"

Duke Griffen nodded.

Duchess Elinor said with contempt, "I think Countess Benchendorff should have let them in. She's an outsider herself."

Sebastian defended the Patroness of Almacks. "Our ambassador's wife doesn't have much room for maneuver. She has to keep up the ton reputation. Or everyone will become like Beau and run off and do almost anything."

Duke Griffen Naismith smiled, but inside he was laughing. "So, he was going to walk the high wire. He was warming up. Had his calisthenics suit on and everything."

"You mean tights," Duchess Elinor said, her face almost blushing at the costume's revealing nature.

"Indeed, our peers and their peers never approved of Duke Rupert's antics. He's there talking with his mulatto wife, who I understand is a well respectable lady, even if she comes from a marred servant, and deeply hidden West Indies background. There he is, the audience members are watching him. They don't know he's an extra act. His mulatto wife sees this circus girl being roughed about, shaken by her shoulders by a tall gentleman."

"No!" said Sebastian.

"That's horrible," said Duchess Elinor.

"But remember, they, this good fellow, Duke Griffen Naismith, are seeing things from a distance. He does not know she is a doxy. He rushes up to the man and breaks things up."

Duchess Elinor and Sebastian are eating fruit, their eyes riveting fixed on Duke Griffen Naismith's blue eyes.

"Duke Griffen Naismith says, 'Stop treating her like that,' and the viscount replies, 'Who are you commoner? I'm ton and I can speak to anyone as I please.' And Repurt Steedmond, standing there in his oddity, calisthenics suit, looking like a high-wire walker, replies, 'Do you want to settle this in the Norman tradition?' to which the viscount's jaw drops; the doxy is totally surprised a ton has rescued her.' Can you just imagine it?"

They all began belly laughing again.

"See this is why ton should follow tradition," Sebastian urged. "If they did, then things like this would never happen."

Lady Duchess Elinor, concern on her face asked, "What happened next, Duke Griffen?"

"Yes, what happened? As ton to ton, he could have proceeded to a duel."

"Nothing happened," Duke Griffen said, after chewing on another apple square. He watched Sebastian eating another third of grapefruit and he watched his once spinster wife, plunking another grape into her small mouth. 'The viscount vowed to get revenge.' I guess. He was quoted as saying, 'This is not the end of this.'"

"Crikey!" cried Sebastian. "What is our world coming to?"

"Lead in our face makeup," Duchess Elinor ventured forth, cautiously.

"No. No. Not lead. Just unconformity," Duke Griffen concluded.

"I agree, Duke Griffen. Unconformity," Sebastian stated flatly.

"If you conformed, Duke Griffen, we wouldn't be married." She got up in a huff. "You can't believe that, Duke Griffen Naismith."

Duke Griffen Naismith's jaw dropped. He didn't think his wife felt so strongly about Duke Rupert Steedmond's antics. "Do not fret, Duchess Elinor, sweet. I do not mean unconformity in our case."

But his wife had stomped off, leaving a half-eaten grape on the white plate with birch leaves of Saxon blue and Devonshire brown.

Duke Griffen Naismith turned to Sebastian.

Sebastian waved his two hands outward in a helpless, 'I don't know what happened' gesture.

"Women," Duke Griffen said and he picked up the other uncut half of apple and started cutting it into cubes.

"I was going to remain mum about this," Sebastian paused, "Duke Griffen I've heard about this--shall I say a wager, between you and this Duke Rupert fellow." Sebastian paused, as he pushed aside his two grapefruit slices. "Is it true?"

Duke Griffen hesitated. He turned away and slumped in his chair for half a second. Then he straightened his back and faced Sebastian. A Damned Hum is what I say it is?"

"False then."

"A fudge. A fuddle fudge."

"Drunken lie?"

Silence reined between the two friends.

"What if it is true, Seb? I love Duchess Elinor. At first it was a wager, yes. I was full of pride and competitive to a fault back then, three years ago. Call it the Beau Brummell influence." Duke Griffen chuckled, but Sebastian didn't.

"I can't say I've ever approved of the spinster marriage. I thought you could get better. Only recently have I heard about this, rumor. I wanted to tell you the rumor, if it is true, is making its way through the ton."

Duke Griffen remained silent.

"They are also saying you're free of fumbler's hall, as well."

"I can have a child with Duchess Elinor! We've wanted to hold off securing our marriage first. Once you have children, Seb, you'll never see your wife alone again!"

"Being single. I don't know. Probably, what you say is true. I do advise you on stocks, industry, and business matters. You need to straightened, or clear this wager thing up with Lady Duchess Elinor before it turns into a divorce."

"Is it that serious, Seb?"

Sebastian nodded. "Not from her point of view, I speak. But the influence of the ton on women is very strong. I mean we men talk about business, except for the Buea Brummell types. Women--they talk about relationships and love."

Duke Griffen Naismith felt a sense of danger and his honor being reputed.

"Some," Sebastian stated flatly, "Duke Griffen, might even go so far as to say you're in fumblers hall because--well--your wife won't let you near her."

"Nasty jar in either case. Seb, all right. I'll clear it up with Duchess Elinor."

"One last thing, Duke Rupert Steedmond has vowed to win this bet and the man's desperate, losing all his associates. Ton will have no more major distractions with the Beau "entertainment" gone to France. "I'm telling you this as a friend, Duke Griffen. To safeguard your marriage, and I believe you truly love Duchess Elinor, you need to be stop paying attention to yourself. How you regard others, paying attention to others, may very well, spell the success or end of your own marriage."

"Sabotage!"

Sebastian nodded. "I don't know the fellow." Sebastian got up to leave. He put on his collapsible black top hat on. He checked his red fob watch, and adjusted his barrel knot cravat. "You know the fellow. Think of what he might do to ruin your marriage and win this bet."

"Thank you, Seb. I appreciate it."

Duke Griffen Naismith's face developed into one of those master portraits' painters paint, after the subject has long lost the ability to smile. He wanted to clear the air. He needed to gather the right words. Everything, if what Sebastian said was true, required it. Duke Griffen sat and thought. "What do I say to a woman who is convinced no one wanted to marry her?"

***

Duchess Elinor cried in her bedroom, the master bedroom.
"Sweet. Unlock the door. I want to talk."

"Go away! I hate you! You never loved me! You loved nothing, but to make money off me!" Duchess Elinor sobbed.

"This isn't true. Not the way you heard it. We're not in fumbler's hall and you are not mad at me. You and I love one another. We're the best relationship the ton ever saw."

"No Marchioness Ava and Marquess Maxwell York are the best relationship the ton ever saw."

"They don't live in London. We do."

"I'm moving back home to Hampshire."

"Duchess, you haven't lived in Hampshire for eight years!' Duke Griffen rattled the door. "Our peers and their peers expect us go on loving one another?"

"Why?" Duchess Elinor screamed. "You diddled me out of my dowry. You diddled me out of my self-respect!" She sobbed. She banged on the blossom pink silk sheet covers. "I had self-respect as a spinster! Self-respect, Duke Griffen Naismith!"

"You'll have self-respect when I win this bet!"

"I won't! I'll never have the ton's respect now. I might as well move to France!"

"We'll get through this. Duke Rupert Steedmond doesn't want his mulatto wife. I can tell you that. He's isolated. He'll quit soon. All he needs is for us to quit before him."

"You only care about yourself, Duke Griffen Naismith. All about you isn't it!"

Duke Griffen Naismith fell silent for a minute. "I was young brash, stupid. I choose his wife and he choose mine. I got the better bargain."

"I'll never let you inside of me again! No children. With no children, I'll retain my self-respect." She sobbed quietly as Duke

Griffen stood outside the door, his hands at his side. He started unwrapping his cravat. "Let me in Duchess Elinor!"

"No!"

"Let me in now!"

"Or else what!" she screamed.

Duke Griffen Naismith rattled the door harder and harder. He stopped himself from banging on it, as Duchess Elinor sat on the bed, waiting pensively to defend herself.

Duke Griffen regained control over his emotions. He backed away from the door. "I'll be in the parlor, my sweet Duchess. We can talk in there. If you want divorce, I'll have, Seb, write up the papers."

Duke Griffen Naismith sat in the parlor the rest of the day. He sat in the parlor the rest of the night. He slept in the parlor for two weeks. Duchess Elinor refused to let him back in the bedroom. She sent her woman servant shopping for her; meals were brought to her. Duchess Elinor read her favorite books, Wordsworth, Helen Maria Williams, Henry Blake, and the Lover's Vow play and even laughed when the woman servant mentioned the crazy antics of Beau Brummell in France.

However, none of these things moved Duchess Elinor to come out of the room or unlock the door when Duke Griffen stood outside it. She even let her food get cold.

What kind of man bets on his wife and let's another man pick his wife? What kind of rake does that? Why and how did he and Duke Rupert Steedmond live with themselves day after day, month after month, year after year, knowing what they had done? Life meant something more to Duke Griffen Naismith, every passing moment now. He grew out of his self-complacency and self-awareness. Beau Brummell cared too much about others bringing him to ruin. Duke Griffen acknowledged it was a long, long time ago when he made the infamous wager. It might require a long, longtime in the future to repair his marriage.

His one advantage, he truly loved Duchess Elinor. Even as

she aged; he loved her. Internally, Duchess Elinor's beauty shined through. They had so much in common. Arranged marriages workedout in the past, he'd tell Duchess Elinor, his sweet. Those marriages lasted because people based them on needed qualities, practicalities, not the fleeting whims of emotions. Theirs's was sort of an arranged marriage. God must have been present in the wedding church and when they consummated their love, because throughout everything, some days, Duke Griffen Naismith forgot all about the bet. He simply loved his wife for who she was inside, not for who she was becoming on the outside. He'd tell Duchess Elinor this when they agreed to meet in the parlor. Yes. Yes.

***

Duchess Elinor chortled. She hadn't had so much fun in years, cooped up as she was in the master bedroom. She didn't wear her corsets or the two linked key engraved whalebone busk in the front of her corset that kept her from bending over. Her belly breathed freely, without any restrictions. Her limbs remained free and subtle. Her very blood cruised from head to toe unencumbered. Mostly, she wore a shift and petticoat and slippers.

The dark rings around her blue eyes went away after the woman servant placed crushed ice, wrapped in a towel, on them. Her emotions had drained through her tearful eyes. Her mind exhausted itself seeking solution to recover her respectability. What else remained, but for her soul to shine forth. She was Duchess Elinor, a respectable woman and one who loved God. Others can do wild things in the bedroom like the Devonshire House Circle, but Duchess Elinor refused their path. One husband-one wife remained Duchess Elinor's plan. Repair her marriage came first. Let God repair her reputation. Then ask God to help she and Duke Griffen Naismith bear a little boy or girl or both. The big manor house felt rather lonely, when the two of them were apart. And it had been a long six weeks.

Time to patch things up.

CHAPTER 4

NEW LEAMINGTON TOWN PRIOR
NORTH SIDE OF LEAMING RIVER
ROYAL PUMP ROOM BATHS
AFTERNOON, MONDAY, JULY 15, 1816

"We were laughing speechless," Duke Rupert Steedmond started off, sitting beside his fully pregnant Duchess Mulatto wife.

She raised her eyebrows whenever something surprised her and she spoke about it. "I couldn't believe it myself," Constantia said wiping off her brow the soothing mineral waters off with her pale-yellow primrose, Primula vulgaris towel.

They laughed hard.

Both were wrapped in the pale-yellow towels, because Duchess Constantia said, Primula vulgaris, was the perfect daywear color for the fashionable.

Duke Rupert asserted, "Oh how I wanted to be there flickering in Beau Brummell's face as he boarded the boat for France. Oh, how I wanted to be there."

The socialite woman next to Duchess Constantia giggled. "They say he was drunk and singing, too." She grinned like a Cheshire Cat. "My ears refused, at first, to take in the good news!"

"It's true," Duke Rupert Steedmond said. "I vowed not to take another slander or cut direct from anyone, and God sent me Buck Brummell, the most well-dressed dandy in England. I said to Brummell, the Prince and certain other aristocrats have taken a serious interest in a fellow with a certain exquisite propriety, with huge debts.' He stopped in his tracks. He lost his repartee wit. His eyes went wide and then he left without a word." Duke Rupert Steedmond's jaw dropped, showing his shocking surprise.

Leaning her head forward before she spoke, Duchess Constantia continued, "Next thing, I hear the arbiter elegantiarum of the ton, fled to France."

All three of them chuckled and chortled. Duke Rupert Steedmond chortling the loudest was throwing his head back in euphoric laughter.

"And Grace Wilson, our reputation and honor received a boost," Duchess Constantia bellowed.

"Although officially, none of what you've heard, Grace, every happened. No one knows what makes a man of such exquisite taste and high connections seek fortunes abroad."

"They shall catch up with him," Grace Wilson replied eagerly. "Rude and vicious men collect their bad karma, too."

"I do get your meaning, Grace. And there is a bit of Beau Brummell in my old friend Duke Griffen Naismith. I have neither seen nor heard a word from him in almost a year."

"That a cut indirect," Grace affirmed.

"I thought so," commented Duchess Constantia wrapping the pale-yellow towel around her six-month huge belly.

She looked almost white in the Primula vulgaris towel. Her slightly plump lips, dark hair, and brown eyes the only hints, perhaps that she belonged to another race or was from Spain or Italy. She felt completed contented and at ease now the pressure fell onto someone else in the ton. Her and Duke Rupert relaxed in their promenade through Hyde Park. Businessmen in the Exchange Building and in the SoHo, district spoke to Duke Rupert Steedmond. Even Bartistu John stopped badgering Duke Rupert to learn Bartitsu fighting to protect himself and his mulatto wife. Circus Jim absence remained a vexing concern, but Duke Rupert Steedmond let the matter slide. He had other plans. If everyone was going to use the doxies at the Circus Jim's, so would he. And already, as he listened in to various ton conversations at country dances, social club get-togethers like at White Club, he heard Duke Griffen Naismith and Duchess Elinor soon verged on a break up. Duke Rupert Steedmond didn't have Brummell ability to turn an ordinary circumstance into an extraordinary one, but Duke Rupert's political sense allowed him to manipulate things behind the scenes with just as much flare and finesse.

Duke Rupert Steedmond had long sense giving up attacking the ton directly, defending his wife directly, asking them to accept his wife as their own. Now he accepted their refusal as a fact. Ton lack of support became his rallying cry to push forward for totally victory in the wager, of three years ago with Duke Griffen Naismith. In his gut, Duke Rupert Steedmond assumed, Duke Griffen, forgot all about the wager. Satisfied with his respectable, albeit aged spinster bride, Duke Griffen got the better of the bet. Until now, and Duke Rupert's whisper campaign against Duke Griffen and Duchess Elinor had one more tactic to spring. One more trap planned ahead. Duke Rupert contacted the Circus Girl and employed her to gather information on Duke Griffen and his Duchess. This circus girl jumped at the opportunity to earn easy money, doing little more than telling Duke Rupert what his archenemy did during the day. During the night, Duke Rupert figured Duke Griffen did the respectable thing: he stayed with his wife and did not whore around for a mistress like the Devonshire House Circle of old.

Finally, this Circus Girl simply made her presence known to Duke Griffen Naismith. At the right moment, which had not come yet, according to Duke Rupert Steedmond's strategic analysis? She'll fall into his hands, and wanting a supple and younger, terribly pretty thing, as Circus Girl was, Duke Griffen Naismith's own self-awareness would be shattered.

Duke Rupert didn't even want to know the Circus Girl's name. "Don't tell me your name. It's unimportant. What's important is that we meet at a small tavern called the Lucky Irish, every Thursday at seven in the evening. Duke Rupert Steedmond always managed an excuse to go for a walk at this time. Duchess Constantia prized this as her reading hour. Duke Rupert would read, too, only his reading took him outdoors to the Lucky Irish Tavern.

Sure, Duke Rupert Steedmond long ago gave up being who he truly was. He needed to be other things to be in the ton anyway.

Some part of him remained true. He loved Duchess Constantia, for the most part. He loved her internally, that was the most important part. Only her skin color vexed him, them both. Everything else of Duchess Constantia became ton. The more ton she became the more Duke Rupert Steedmond wanted her accepted as ton!

He successfully avoided the suggestion, their marriage spawned from a bet, a bachelor's wager, replying, "I cannot recall something done during a drunken moment of my youth. Do you remember every statement you made at a crush or a rout?"

To be fair, as the woman servant for Countess Heathcote, in her past life, Duchess Constantia didn't officially attend many crushes or rout or so-called parties. She, therefore, had no impulsive comments to make at said routs, crushes, or parties. But it was enough to satisfied Duchess Constantia. All she cared about was giving birth to her children and settling into her good fortune of having made a good marriage--to a Duke. She went from cucumberish to possessing a huge dowry; Duke Rupert Steedmond wrote his will specifically for her, but the annuity would most like become hers should anything happen to him.

Duchess Constantia laughed at the private joke of Grace Wilson about dancing. "No. I can't dance a jig now. I can't even see my feet now!" Her life turned better and better, now that the snubs and cut directs and even cut indirect stopped. She went from servant to Duchess. The perfect Cinderella story read to her, like many girls hoped for, materialized for Duchess Constantia. And her bob-cull husband showed her only pleasantness. What more did a girl want out of life, besides to be on the right side of God himself?

CHAPTER 5

HYDE PARK
QUIETER SECTION
LONDON, ENGLAND
AFTERNOON, THURSDAY, AUGUST 1, 1816

She wore Turkey red, because of the country the color originated from. Diagonal cone shaped half-inch strips in the color decorated the cotton dress, with elaborate shaped sleeves. No other woman wore such fabrics yet, as they were new. The man who purchased it for her Rupert Steedmond insisted on her wearing this dress and no other, not by accident or mistake. The Hyde Park man likes Turkey red, Duke Rupert Steedmond insisted.

Circus Girl, Olivia Eggleston, pressed the new cotton fabric dress down her slender, shapely figure, as she walked alone in Hyde Park, carrying a small basket. Following the man for weeks enabled her to afford a good apartment. The man seemed good enough, proper. This would be the last time, she followed Duke Griffen Naismith. Also, Duke Rupert Steedmond insisted, she carry it, and as far as Olivia figured, it was something ton like. All she needs do was when seeing Duke Griffen Naismith, she was to leave the basket at his feet before planting a big kiss on Duke Griffen Naismith's lips. Then Duke Rupert Steedmond said, he'd meet her at the Irish Tavern at their usual time, and give her the ship tickets to America, and the ship sailing that day. He showed her the purchased tickets.

America. America. America filled Olivia's mind. No more being mistaken for a doxy. No more being thought of as lower class, in America they abolished all that ton stuff. She can be free. Joyful, smiling, blissfully unaware, many people walked in Hyde Park, but Duke Griffen Naismiths did not yet. Circus Girl, not in this section, Duke Griffen Naismith's section. You can't miss him.

Olivia promenade slowly into the quieter section of Hyde Park. She looked left and right. People paid little attention to her and Olivia attributed this to the basket. When Duke Griffen Naismith and Duchess Elinor came into view, Olivia found herself in a near panic. But then she thought of her new life in America. I must do this. I need my freedom. He was ton and he had resources and wealth, what harm could she do, he, Duke Griffen Naismith, could not undo. After all, she was a harmless little girl from the country. In her mind, the kiss on the lips bothered her a bit, though. She might not do that part. She didn't know. All she wanted to do was leave England and the ton and men who frequented the circus and mistook her for something she was not.

"I'm glad we put that beside us. And don't fret, my Duchess Elinor, sweet. You're mine. Our peers and their peers know this, unequivocally."
"Duke Griffen Naismith. I thought you were lying. But--your honesty these past few weeks. The bet means nothing to me now. I don't care because; you never played around on me. Sebastian vouched for you." Duchess Elinor believed in her Duke Griffen Naismith. She never stopped loving him, never. All of the ton women rallied around Duchess Elinor, and none had a bad word to say about Duke Griffen.

Olivia took a big breath. Duke Griffen Naismith's walking stick remained a problem, however. What if he should whack her, thinking of her as roughen. Her big blue eyes batted nervously. The ton couple approached, slowly. Duchess Elinor glanced at Olivia and Olivia glanced back nice as can be. Closer. Closer. She waited until the last second. Olivia dropped the basket which Duke Griffen Naismith promptly put his walking stick inside. Unable to pull it out to defend himself, he turned surprised to look at the girl, Olivia.

She found her mark easy to kiss and went ahead grabbing him about his upper arms, she tiptoed and planted a wet kiss on his lips.

Sending Duke Griffen Naismith's surprised lips moving and welcoming the gesture.

The basket went flying into the air in a big loop circle, as Olivia took off, walking fast, and walking running and as she turned behind a ridge of bushes, walking as if nothing happened.

Few saw the incident. Those who did found it difficult to believe. The basket remained at Duke Griffen Naismith's feet, full of white cloths and muslin fabric. Nothing more. Wiggling his walking stick, Duke Griffen Naismith turned around to see no girl in Turkey red insight.

"Even the ton women can be fooled apparently," Duchess Elinor yelled. "I'll have you divorced as soon as Sebastian can work up the papers."
"But Duchess Elinor. I don't know the lady!"
"She is familiar enough to plant a kiss on your lips."
Duke Griffen Naismith defended himself, "I have never seen her!"
"How does she know we always walk this way, our way, our way from our peers and their peers?"
"I don't know--Duchess. I haven't been seeing anyone for a long, long time."
"You haven't--Duke Griffen Naismith. And the Turkey red. You went on and on about it coming to England."
"Not like this. I meant fashion, style, Duchess Elinor."

Duchess Elinor stormed off, upset, and leaving any joyful memories of their reunion scattered about like the white cloth of surrender on the Hyde Park grass.

Duke Griffen rose up his hands in a helpless gesture of defeat. "Here I bring us back from a breakup and now we break up." Duke Griffen looked around at the ground. He spotted something peculiar knitted in gold on the white cloth. "Surrender."

***

SOHO SECTION
LUCKY IRISH TAVERN
LONDON, ENGLAND
SEVEN IN EVENING, THURSDAY, AUGUST 1, 1816

Olivia came into the crowded tavern wearing a white empire dress with black trim, and white slipper shoes. The men all looked at her, but the bartender shook his head no and the crowd turned away. Olivia sauntered up to the bartender and placed one of the small white cloths, folded in a triangle on the bar. He snatched it up and nodded to his right. Walking to her left, Olivia noticed all the cutout newspaper faces, politicians on the wall of the tavern. The bartender knew a lot of people.

In the darker, quieter section of the Lucky Irish tavern, and its few thick, pane windows, Olivia searched two sections down. "There you are!"

"Quiet!" said Duke Rupert Steedmond. "I don't know your name and you don't know mine!" he hissed. "You were successful?"

Olivia replied, "I was."

"I heard you were. I wanted to make sure you kissed him. I had someone watching." Duke Rupert Steedmond slid the ship tickets. Wait five minutes, here. No talking. When the bartender waves, a brogham carriage will come. You get inside it."

"This is no white slavery trick, is it? You give me tickets then turn me into a sex slave."

"Everything is legitimate. I have men watching. You will be on that ship tonight at 8 p.m. No turning back now, little Miss Circus Muffet. You wanted the Cinderella life. This is the cost. Aloneness until you reach America. Talk to no one. Your meals have been paid for. You're going to see your granddad, in New York."

"My grandad in New York?" Olivia became happily and scared. She took a big breath. "What happens when I reach America?"

"I'll have a friend of mine; I can trust get you a job as a

seamstress. You can do it. It's not turning flips or somersaults in the Jim's Circus. Rather boring work, twelve hours, but you can survive off the salary."

"Crikey! You are like the good, dad. The one I never had."

Olivia turned when Duke Rupert Steedmond pointed to the bartender. She got up and said goodbye. "I may have done a bad thing, but I pray for God to forgive me. My life seemed headed for danger the longer I stayed in the circus. Sorry, I wasn't supposed to speak."

Duke Rupert Steedmond gave a curt nod.

Olivia didn't look at the men in the bar. Remaining invisible became her primary goal from here on out, until she reached America. Once outside, the black brougham carriage seemed to open magically. Olivia, the former Circus Girl, looked carefully all inside the dark pristine interior. She grinned and stepped inside.

The cool seats and smooth ride felt exciting. Each turn the carriage driver took his time on. Nothing seemed rushed about the trip to the shipyard. Turning to glance outside the right and then left window, she remained seated against the back, anonymous, as Duke Rupert Steedmond said. Inside the carriage above the opposite seat was a black box in the far corner. She almost missed it. She stared at it until the gold lettering flashed when they traveled under one of the many gaslights in London. "Olivia Eggleston." Suddenly taken by the surprise, she slowly reached over for it and put it onto her lap. The note on top, a beige calling card read, for Olivia Eggleston.

Hesitating. Thinking something bad waited to destroy her dreams, she paused. Then taking the risk, Olivia opened it.

"Inside this box are one, papers announcing you as my niece from London, England. Two, you will find a small dowry worth L200. Three, you will find I understand the risk you took today. In return, I will see you do well in America, Niece. But our activities in this matter with Duke Griffen Naismith must remain a secret. Is that clear?"

Olivia read the final part. Signed, Duke Rupert Steedmond.

Olivia boarded the ship, which shall remain unknown and sailed to America. Being the smart girl, as she was, she took the job and took some college education and improved her life in progressive steps.

CHAPTER 6

WHITE CLUB
NOS. 37-38 ST. JAMES'S STREET
UPPER GAMESTER ROOM
FOUR O'CLOCK AFTERNOON, SATURDAY, AUGUST 31, 1816

Duke Rupert Steedmond sat around a large oval table waiting for his victim, the loser on the bet.

"I do say, it is a bit strange, you won this bet, Duke Rupert Steedmond," said one of the many Earls in attendance.

"Yes," replied another duke. "Your wife being a mulatto seemed in unconquerable disadvantage."

"Yes, and his spinster wife, ahem, former wife, knew all of ton matters, traditions and such," added a Marquess, who bet a lot but paid all his lost debts in a speedy time frame.

A man rushed into the upper room, a young count with black hair. "Here it is the official divorce papers, from the lawyers." He slapped the paper on the oval table. He tapped it twice.

One of the men in their white cravats, black coat, and tails, quickly slid the paper before him. "Aha, Sebastian signature. That's it," commented a Duke from North Yorkshire.

"Amazing feat," Duke Rupert Steedmond.

"Frankly, I didn't think you had it in you. Griffen Naismith is a very determined ton fellow."

"He fought a Battle Royal to keep his marriage intact, I bet."

"Aye, in his youth, Griffen Naismith took some boxing training from Gentlemen Jackson."

"The sordid thing about this whole affair--" the young Earl from Dorset began and paused.

Duke Rupert Steedmond hesitated. He knew no one

discovered his ruse. He was especially careful. He took advantage of the pause. "Don't worry, Griffen Naismith will arrive gentlemen."

Everyone laughed.

"I lost my train of thought for a second," commented the young Earl. "Even though it was in the rules, our peers and their peers would judge the outcome, we fellows didn't get a chance to bet on the event."

"Yeah, yeah!" all the ton members of England present commented.

Duke Rupert Steedmond chortled. "I do get your meaning, but see, you did vote. After the terms were set, I came back two weeks later and put a mysterious bet into the black betting book."

"That mysterious wager?"

"The one called 'Mysterious Bet'," replied Duke Rupert. "I am bet number two; Griffen is bet number one."

All the ton members thought back. "I remember it," said a Duke from Wales.

"Give me that betting book," said the Marquess from Cornwall. "Does feel a bit lighter with Beau Brummell not putting in bets he can't pay off."

Burst of laughter, some deep, some softer, some shorter, erupted from the ton crowd.

"As I was saying," the Marquess of Cornwall continued, and he flipped backward several pages. "There it is. Mysterious Bet One or Mysterious Bet Two."

"So, we did get in on the bet!"

"Crikey! What did I wager, or upon whom did I wager?" asked the young Earl from Dorset.

Marquess of Cornwall slid his forefinger down the page. "You did well. Fifty pounds."

Young Earl of Dorset raised his fist in celebration.

"What a sight! What a sight!" Marquess of Cornwall turned the betting book around. "Look at all these bets on Duke Griffen Naismith."

Speaking a duke said, "He was such a cocky, fellow three years ago."

"Marriage settled him. All that struggling free of fumblers hall. I guess."

The men laughed in another uproar.

Duke Rupert Steedmond chortled. "I should think, with less on his mind, Duke Griffen will sire, a brood of children with his next, younger wife."

Noise of guffaws and festive laughter filled the upper gamester room in White Club on St. James Street.

The door opened suddenly and Duke Griffen Naismith appeared. His eyes pinkish-red. His jaw twitching. A growl caught in his throat but clearly on his face, as his angry eyes scanned the room of ton men. He spotted Duke Rupert Steedmond and moved to the front of the oval table.

Viewing Duke Rupert Steedmond's state of mind and face, all the ton members fell silent.

In the twinkling of an eye, Duke Griffen pulled from his coat and tails jacket an English blunderbuss, capable of firing multiple projectiles in a single shot. Wooden body and flaring steel nozzle pointed directly at Duke Rupert Steedmond.

All the ton members pushed their chairs back, most standing abruptly, to get out of the English blunderbuss's aim.

Duke Rupert sat calmly. "Is this how you want our peers and their peers to see you Duke Griffen? Hurt, sorrowful, slovenly in your attitude toward a fellow ton."

Duke Griffen Naismith's twisted face showed pure anger. "I won't be run out of England like Beau Brummell."

"I mean. I do get your meaning bringing a gun. Perhaps, I'd have brought cannon myself."

Ton men felt more relaxed and chuckled quietly.

"But, Duke Griffen, no one is talking about running you out of England," Duke Rupert waved his hands wide apart. "It's all a sport, good fellow, just a wager. We, ton, bet about all sorts of things; sometimes life-and-death matters." Duke Rupert pointed to Duke Griffen, "You, too. You are one of us."

"Yes, Duke Griffen Naismith. You are still one of us," commented the Marquess who always paid his debt quickly.

"I loved my spinster wife!" Duke Griffen blared at the men. "You, ton, men lose sight of the severity of things, with all your betting and cocky boasting of who is better than whom."

"And you Duke Griffen were the best among us at that betting," said an older Count with large bushy white sideburns and a thick matching mustache that curled into handlebars.

"Fair enough criticism," said the young Earl, very close to the English blunderbuss still pointing at Duke Rupert. "Yet, some of us still value marriage. I want to be married. I was very glad at your marriage to the spinster of Hampshire. I bet a lot on you to win."

None of the men said anything about this Banbury Tale. All of them wanted to escape unharmed, with their lives.

"Me, too," commented a count.
"Yeah, I did as well," said a Duke

Duke Griffen turned, briefly, to the young Earl. Then Duke Griffen turned back furious at Duke Rupert. "Duke Rupert Steedmond used subterfuge to win the bet. He sent a woman to tempt me."

"Well if one falls for temptation--" started one ton member before Duke Griffen cut him off.

"She kissed me. Unawares and surprising me in Hyde Park."

"Gosh, man, you had your walking stick. Why didn't you just block her?" asked a viscount from London.

"Because--because it got stuck in her lunch basket."

"Her lunch basket!"

"Her lunch basket!"

"Do you mean to say a strange woman accosted you with her picnic basket and unarmed you, Duke Griffen."

Now, all the ton men laughed uproariously.

Duke Rupert Steedmond smiled, and chuckled.

Duke Griffen Naismith, realizing how stupid the whole thing sound, began to find the situation sportive and amusing. He let out a short laugh. As he was a smile and smug fellow when happy, that appearance returned to his face. "Yes. She caught me off guard," said Duke Griffen, lowering his English blunderbuss. "Quite the witty trick, I must say, Duke Rupert."

"I cannot account for rare events. Sometimes a falling star passes us in the night, but many more in the day, and we see them not."

"Here, here!"

"It's all a joke, my wager, Duke Griffen Naismith. Forget it man."

"No one will run you out of England," said the Marquess of

Cornwall. "I'm scratching off my bet on Duke Rupert. Because you loved your spinster wife."

"Give me that betting book said another ton member. "I bet on Duke Rupert, too. Love is more important in my book. No one has to pay me."

Several ton members scratched their winning bets off the White Club betting book.

Duke Rupert Steedmond chortled. "Duke Griffen Naismith, I bet on you to win."

"But why?" Duke Griffen Naismith asked. "I didn't bet on you to win."

"Because I said to myself your marriage choice for me brought me such, joy; how could I collect on a bet on myself. I already won the best thing a man wants in life. A loving, exciting, trustworthy wife."

Duke Griffen considered these words and fought back tears. Many years, he wanted a good wife, and sure Duchess Elinor wasn't what he had in mind, but he loved her immensely. Now he realized Duke Rupert Steedmond felt in a similar fashion about his mulatto wife. The two men did each other a favor. How devastated Duke Griffen felt about his divorce. He tried to explain over and over and over, the random event, the picnic basket girl, was planned.

Duke Griffen's former Duchess Elinor found such a thing preposterous. One man stooped to such low heights to bring another man into divorce. Divorce from the woman that man loved. Even explaining the betting book and White Club and ton male competition wasn't enough. Duke Griffen's Duchess left him nonetheless.

"I admit. After winning, I planned to thank you as well. To my new thinking, there is no such thing as a spinster. My former Duchess had all the flexibility, prowess, and passion any man wanted. We held off having children to enjoy our state of bliss longer. Perhaps, we held off too long." Duke Griffen lowered the English blunderbuss, used by stagecoach drivers, pirates for its deadly efficiently. "If we married and had a child, the divorce required more time to work out."

"I am truly sorry, for the events you encountered, Duke Griffen Naismith."

"And I am sorry for any trouble I caused you, Duke Rupert Steedmond." Duke Griffen paused. "I'll pay all my debts."

The Marquess of Cornwall started doing the calculations. "With the scratched off bets, and your considerable funds, Duke Griffen, you won't have to run off to England after all," commented the Marquess joking.

Every ton member in the room laughed; those who scratched off their bets, those who lied about their bets and those who collected on their bets.

Duke Griffen Naismith grew boisterous for once. "A round of drinks on me!"

"That's a sport, Duke Griffen."
"Here! Here!" said the Duke from North Yorkshire.

So, the ton, men exchanged betting papers; people paid up. They all laughed and drank until the meal was served at six o'clock. Fine memories and happiness abound in the room. Friendships deepened as they gossiped and waited for the bill to be served at nine o'clock. Life returned to normal. Duke Griffen Naismith and Duke Rupert Steedmond shook hands forgiving all. White Club regained its sense of power and freedom and adventure to the men, like it held in the past, even before and after Beau Brummell ruled it.

One hour passed, two hours, and the meal done and completed, the ton men relaxed. They took off their coat and tails and many of them had a smoke on their Cuban cigars. And this is how the story would have ended except for one more interruption.

When the White Club upper door burst open again, two women stood there in their Pomona green Empire dresses, their hair in tight buns, and both holding an English blunderbuss pistols on the men. Although Duchess Constantia's Pomona green Empire dress stretched to its limit under her nine-month-old belly.

"Crikey! Duchess Constantia what are you doing!"
"Duchess Elinor, please, don't shoot. I know I planned on getting revenge, but we work it all out!"
"That may be fine and well for you ton men to have sports playing with our lives," Duchess Elinor replied, "but we women want in on the fun, too."
Duchess Constantia practically rested the blunderbuss pistol on her pregnant belly. "In the old West Indies days, women pirates existed," started Duchess Constantia. "Women pirates used to carry English blunderbuss because a woman's capture meant rape and torture. Perhaps you gentlemen felt an inkling for the old wild days, and created this White Club," the mulatto Duchess waved her blunderbuss at the ton men. All the ton men scrambled back against the walls. The two men whose wives suddenly commanded the room felt weak and helpless as children.

None of this figured in Duke Rupert Steedmond's estimation of his wife's reactions.
Neither did Duke Griffen Naismith guess his wife indignation at the trick on her affections.

"Women, however, see love as sacred, gentlemen," said former Duchess Elinor.
"I quite agree, women do see love as sacred, gentlemen," added Duchess Constantia.
"You want adventure. Bet on your own lives. Who wants to bet, our blunderbuss pistols will miss your bodies?" asked former Duchess Elinor.
"No takers?" taunted Duchess Constantia.

Silence.

Duchess Constantia asked, "What we want to know is who won the bet?"
"Yes, please tell us who won the bet, of Our Peers and their

Peers?" said former Duchess Elinor.

"No one won the bet!" Duke Rupert Steedmond exclaimed.
"We called off, scratched off our bets," Duke Griffen Naismith explained.

"No one won! Then why are you all celebrating and happy?" former Duchess Elinor asked.
Duchess Constantia nodded. "Please do tell us about all this festive happiness I see."

The men found themselves held captive to the buttocks and tongue of Duke Rupert Steedmond and Duke Griffen Naismith's wives. The scolding something they'd never forget. Yet they needed to supply an answer for a woman scorned was a woman hurt. Each man suddenly put themselves in the woman's place. What if their wives bet on them staying married? What if the loser had to pay money for getting a divorce from his wife? Tinkering with these thoughts held captive to their minds by the two English blunderbusses' pointed at their persons, brought about soberness, no lack of wine could inspire.

"This is the betting book," stated Duke Griffen after receiving it from a ton further down the large oval table. "You can see Duchess Elinor. My bets are crossed off. Duke Rupert Steedmond crossed off his bet to me. Several bets are crossed off, because we men felt ashamed at destroying the love lives of Duke Rupert Steedmond and me. I love you Duchess Elinor, former Duchess. I still want us to get married now that this sordid betting book wager is over. We crossed off our bets to one another because; we were totally pleased with our choices. God brought about this event to bring us together, Duchess Elinor."

"Yes, Duchess Constantia. I love you, even with all the problems; I loved you with all my soul. You made me so happy. I wished we met somehow--but--this is how God works, in mysterious ways."

All the ton men repeated, "In mysterious ways."

Duchess Constantia blinked her eyes, "I found myself in tears realizing Duchess Elinor and Duke Griffen divorced. I sought her out and said, we will end this matter. We will show these men love is nothing to trifle with. Love is real."

"Love is true and necessary," former Duchess Elinor said, "in a world revolving around business of winning, taking and getting, affection between man and woman symbolizes the greater love God has for us all, men and women."

"Here! Here!" said one of the ton members.
"Here! Here!" said all the ton men.

Duchess Elinor lowered her English blunderbuss and put it inside her silver linked purse.

Duchess Constantia blinked again, and as every male ton member waited for her to lower her English blunderbuss, she started blinking faster. Leaning her head forward as if to speak again, she fell downward, backward and the gun went off as she hit the floor.

Every ton man ducked.

Luckily, no one was hurt. Several holes hit the ceiling of the upper White Club room. Duchess Elinor tried to stop Duchess Constantia from falling, but being nine months pregnant, Duchess Constantia's weight was, too, much. She slumped to the floor.

Duke Rupert Steedmond cried out! "Duchess Constantia! Crikey! Someone gets a doctor!"
Duchess Elinor took the blunderbuss out of Duchess Constantia's open hand.
Duke Rupert Steedmond knelt and held his mulatto wife. "Is there a doctor in the house?"
The young Earl ran downstairs and cried out, "Is there a doctor in the house."
Duke Griffen Naismith yelled, "Four-hundred ton members

and no doctor?"

The young Earl ran outside and cried, "Is there a doctor nearby? We need a doctor!"

"I'm a doctor!" yelled a man coming out of an upper-class English Tavern on St. James Street.

"We have a pregnant woman, ton. She's having a baby?"

"Take me to her."

***

"Did her water break yet?" the doctor asked.

"No. Not yet," said former Duchess Elinor.

"Thank God! Give me some room, White Club gentlemen! She needs to breath!"

All the ton members back away again, this time not out of fear, but the unknown mystery of childbirth and what to do about it.

In the darken room of White Club Duchess Constantia looked completely white.

The doctor quickly and discreetly examined, Duchess Constantia. "We're not going to have enough time to rush her to the hospital. Gentlemen of White Club, I need to commandeer this room. Out! All of you except Duchess Elinor and Duke Rupert."

The ton members paused, gasps on their faces. Never in their lives had they encounter such events.

"Out of the room," yelled Duke Rupert and Duke Griffen at the same time. "Out of the room!"

"That means you, too, darling. My love. My husband!"

"Elinor, you still want to marry me again!"

"Of course! All is explained. All have been chastised. All of our honor," former Duchess Elinor looked down to the Duchess Constantia, slowly coming to consciousness again, "has been regained."

After the ton men left the room. Quietness took over for a

moment.

"Help me lift her up to the table Duke Rupert Steedmond.'"
On the oval table, Duchess Constantia's water broke.
The doctor commented, "There goes her water. We don't have long now."
"She said, her family always has successful births," Duke Rupert Steedmond replied.

The doctor standing between Duchess Constantia's spread legs reached to pull out his forceps.
"Doctor!" Duchess Constantia cried. "It's coming out!"
The doctor dropped the forceps from his hands, spread his fingers turned around just in time for the baby's head and shoulder to come out. He caught the little boy child in his hands. "I guess forceps are not necessary." He chuckled.
"I do get your meaning, doctor," Duke Rupert Steedmond replied. "Honestly love, why didn't you tell me to take you to the hospital?"
"All that time in the mineral baths made the birth easier, I guess. Besides, I had some unfinished business," she turned to Duchess Elinor. "Keeping love in the forefront of our lives, you and I and Duke Griffen Naismith and Duchess Elinor."

***

Duchess Constantia had a healthy boy. She and Duke Rupert Steedmond went on to have two girls. They stayed in north London and lived happily, but Duke Rupert Steedmond no more attended the White Club, or walked on the high wire, being a mature ton man. He and the Duchess Constantia did attend the Ascot horseraces, though.

Duchess Elinor had a healthy girl, and then a healthy boy and girl twins, proving spinsterhood was a slur. Duke Griffen Naismith also did not frequent White Club and he ceased betting on all things. They remarried. Duke Griffen Naismith and Duchess Elinor and went on to have a pleasant time, walking in Hyde Park and living in southern London.

Duchess Constantia and Duchess Elinor became best friends; Duke Rupert and Duke Griffen became best friends. The ton members of society forgot all about the drama of betting and wagers that engulfed them. Even Lady Countess Dorothea Benchendorff agreed to let Duke Rupert and Duchess Constantia into the Assembly's of Almack dances for the remaining season.

Olivia worked as a seamstress until she put herself through school. After college she went on to become a schoolteacher for young children. She married and birthed two children. After becoming a teacher and secure, she cut off all contacts with Duke Rupert Steedmond.

--THE END--

Notes

Printed in Great Britain
by Amazon